W9-BAX-684

Sleepyhead

Sleepy

Karma Wilson and

head

JOHN SEGAL

Margaret K. McElderry Books   New York   London   Toronto   Sydney

Sleepyhead, Sleepyhead.

Good night, good night,

my Sleepyhead.

Your teeth are
brushed,

your book is

read.

Go to sleep. It's time for bed.

One
more
book,
says Sleepyhead.

Sleepyhead,
Sleepyhead.

Sweet dreams,

sweet dreams,

my Sleepyhead.

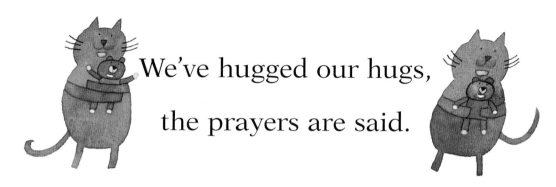

We've hugged our hugs,
the prayers are said.

Go to sleep. It's time for bed.

One
more
hug,

says Sleepyhead.

Sleepyhead, Sleepyhead.
Now close your eyes,
my Sleepyhead.

We've kissed our kiss, your quilt is spread.

Go to sleep. It's time for bed.

One
more
kiss,

says Sleepyhead.

Sleepyhead,
Sleepyhead.
The moon is
HIGH,
my Sleepyhead.

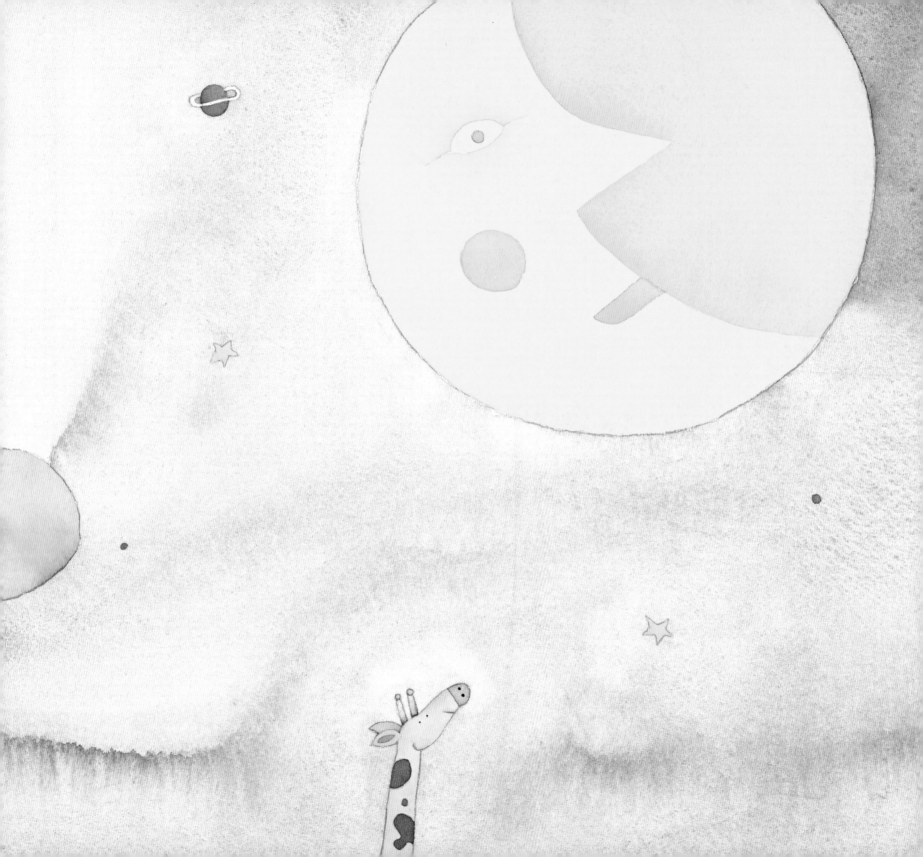

You've drunk your drink, *Good night, I said.* Go to sleep.

It's time for bed.

One more drink,
says Sleepyhead.

And . . .

One more teddy, one more snuggle. One more comfy, cozy cuddle.

Just
one
more,

says Sleepyhead.

I promise

then

I'll go

to bed.

One more story said just right, one more gaze upon the night.

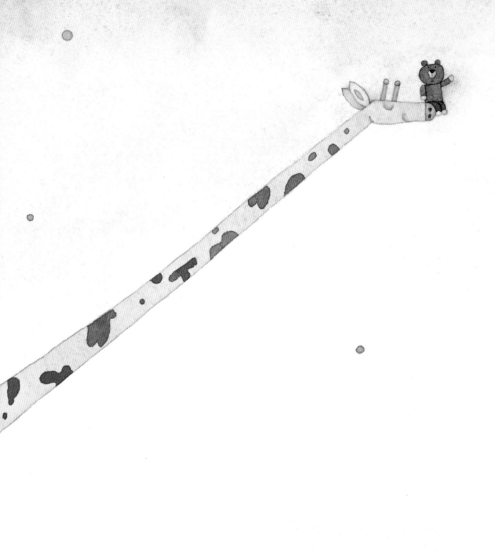

Just one more,

says Sleepyhead.

I promise

then I'll go to bed.

One more blanky piled on.

One more stretch
and one more

yawn. . . .

Just one more,

says Sleepyhead.

I promise

then

I'll go

to bed.

Sleepyhead, Sleepyhead.

Sleep tight, sleep tight,

my Sleepyhead.

Tomorrow's play is just ahead.

I love you so. Now rest your head.

Not

a

word

says

Sleepyhead.

To my Grandpa, who always told me one
more story before tucking me in—K. W.

For Emily and Josh, always—J. S.

Margaret K. McElderry Books
An imprint of Simon & Schuster Children's Publishing Division
1230 Avenue of the Americas, New York, New York 10020

Book design by Ann Bobco
The text for this book is set in New Aster.
The illustrations for this book are rendered in watercolor.
Manufactured in China
10 9 8 7 6 5 4 3 2 1
Library of Congress Cataloging-in-Publication Data
Wilson, Karma.
Sleepyhead / Karma Wilson ; illustrated by John Segal.—1st ed.
p.   cm.
Summary: A kitten helps her favorite teddy bear prepare for bed.
ISBN-13: 978-1-4169-1241-5
ISBN-10: 1-4169-1241-X
[1. Bedtime—Fiction. 2. Cats—Fiction. 3. Stories in rhyme.] I. Segal, John, ill. II. Title.
PZ8.3.W6976Sle 2006
[E]—dc22
2005017243